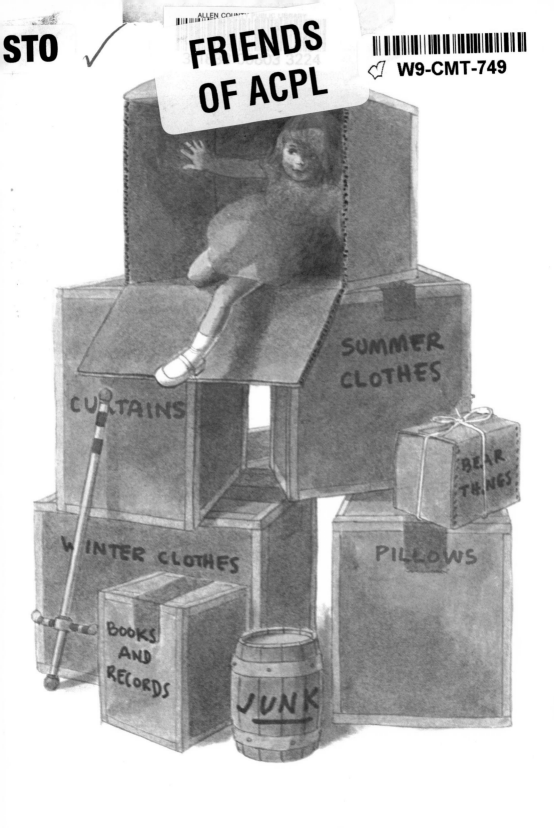

SUMMER
CLOTHES

CURTAINS

BEAR
THINGS

WINTER CLOTHES

PILLOWS

BOOKS
AND
RECORDS

JUNK

moving day

by Tobi Tobias

pictures by William Pène du Bois

Alfred A. Knopf ❧ New York

for John, with low rumblings

This is a Borzoi Book published by Alfred A. Knopf, Inc.

*Text Copyright ©1976 by Tobi Tobias. Illustrations Copyright©1976 by William Pène du Bois.
All rights reserved under International and Pan-American Copyright Conventions. Published in
the United States by Alfred A. Knopf, Inc., New York, and simultaneously in Canada by
Random House of Canada Limited, Toronto. Distributed by Random House, Inc., New York.
Library of Congress Cataloging in Publication Data. Tobias, Tobi. Moving Day. SUMMARY:
A small girl is involved in the excitement, turmoil, and sadness of moving from one house to
another and keeps her toy bear close for reassurance. [1. Moving, Household—Fiction] I. Du
Bois, William Penè, 1916-   II. Title. PZ7.T56Mo [E] 75-22275. ISBN 0-394-83115-2.
ISBN 0-394-93115-7 lib. bdg. Manufactured in the United States of America.*

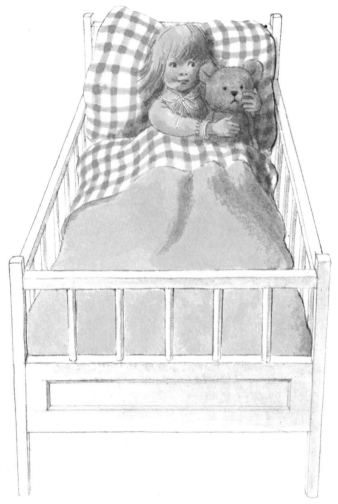

we're moving soon
new house, new home
moving day coming soon
Daddy and Mommy say it's nice
a big new house, far away
Bear's a little scared
not me

getting ready, ready to move
there's a lot we have to do
sort out, throw away

not Bear

remember
keep
give away

save all the things we might need soon

pack up
carefully
toys in here and clothes in there

dishes and pots and pans and pictures

rugs and boots and books and umbrellas

and my pillow
and my lamp
and my bottle cap collection

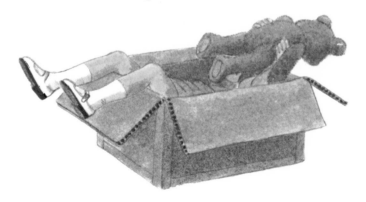

no, don't pack Bear
he stays with me

it's today
it's moving day
we're all packed up
boxes and boxes and boxes
load the van
load the car
boxes, boxes, boxes, boxes

wait—where's Bear?
please find Bear
he's not in the big box

not in the car
not in the house

it's all empty, nothing there
please find Bear
Bear? Bear?

Oh

it's time to say goodbye
goodbye house

goodbye Joey

goodbye street

goodbye, goodbye

I'll come back to visit you
goodbye playground
goodbye trees
Bear says goodbye too

long way to ride
Bear sits with me
houses and trees go whizzing past

buildings and streets go sliding by

riding, riding, riding

Bear takes a little nap

then watches out the window some more
until we stop

here it is
new house, new home
look around
it's very big
and different
from our old one
there's our table and the chairs
same old couch—put different ways

new room, new bed
it's very big
and different
from the one
Bear was used to

rooms and doors and stairs and boxes
unpack, put away
stairs and doors and rooms and boxes
Bear could get lost here
if he's not careful

supper on paper plates
just like a picnic
the things I like best
hamburgers and green peas
and mashed potatoes
milk with a straw
Bear can sit beside me
like always

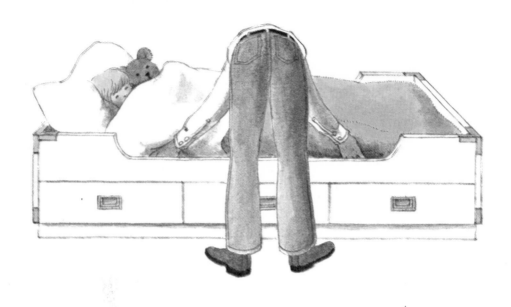

Bear likes the new bed
it's not too big
with him in it
Daddy comes and tucks me tight

out the window
I can see a lot of sky
and the stars
Bear and I hear new noises everywhere
until he falls asleep

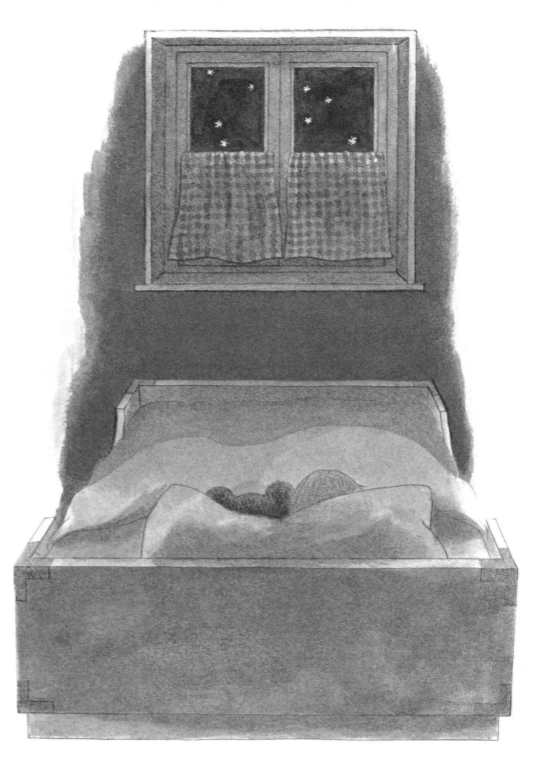

wake up Bear and go and see
new street
new places
new faces

I can ride my bike
all the way down the road
and back
myself
there's a kid who looks like Joey
only different
I think Bear will like it here
new house, new home
goodbye
hello

Tobi Tobias has written a number of books for young people, among them *The Quitting Deal* and *Isamu Noguchi: The Life of a Sculptor*. Her writing on dance appears regularly in *Dance Magazine*, where she is a Contributing Editor, and in *The New York Times*. Ms. Tobias lives with her husband and children in the brownstone they are renovating on New York's Upper West Side.

William Pène du Bois's illustrations, as well as his stories, have long enchanted readers of books for young people. Born in New Jersey, he spent a number of years in New York and now lives in a house that projects into the Mediterranean Sea, near the old port of the city of Nice. There he spends time writing and illustrating books, playing tennis, and competing in vintage car rallies in his 1931 Rolls Royce.